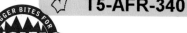

CHOMPS

BIGGER BITES FOR BIGGER READERS!

SCREAM WORLD

Grommet's friends put him
up to things and he falls for it—
every time.

But when he's caught
switching signs at Scream World,
the manager
finds just the right way
to use his talents. That's if he doesn't
get eaten by panthers first.

MORE CHOMPS TO SINK YOUR TEETH INTO!

THE BOY WHO WOULD LIVE FOREVER
Moya Simons

STELLA BY THE SEA
Ruth Starke

THE TWILIGHT GHOST
Colin Thiele

WALTER WANTS TO BE A WEREWOLF
Richard Harland

BIGGER BITES FOR
CHOMPS
BIGGER READERS!

SCREAM WORLD

Prepare for the ride of your life!

James Moloney

RUNNING PRESS
KIDS
PHILADELPHIA·LONDON

For Ben Scott

First published by Penguin Books Australia, 2003
First published in the United States by Running Press Book Publishers, 2007.

Printed in China

9   8   7   6   5   4   3   2   1
Digit on the right indicates the number of this printing

Library of Congress Control Number: 2006929402
ISBN-13: 978-0-7624-2926-4
ISBN-10: 0-7624-2926-7

Original design by David Altheim, Penguin Group (Australia).
Additional design for this edition by Frances J. Soo Ping Chow
Typography: New Century School Book

This book may be ordered by mail from the publisher.
Please include $2.50 for postage and handling.
But try your bookstore first!

This edition published by Running Press Kids, an imprint of
Running Press Book Publishers
2300 Chestnut Street
Philadelphia, PA 19103-4371

Visit us on the web!
www.runningpress.com

Ages 8–12
Grades 3–6

CHAPTER

I'm a sucker for a challenge and that can get me in a bit of strife sometimes. My mother says I'm in with the wrong bunch of friends. She wishes I'd hang out with nice boys who wear their caps the right way round and play chess.

My dad knows what it's like. "You do it for the buzz, don't you, Grommet?" he said, with a man-to-man grin on his face.

"Yeah, I suppose," I answered, grinning back at him.

It was a trap. He was onto me like a ton of

bricks. *Fool, stupid, crazy, irresponsible, wake up to yourself, smile off your face.* He crammed all of these into the first ten seconds.

He was right, of course. I do it for the excitement, just to see if I can pull it off. Skateboards are my weakness. Jump up onto a park bench and slide along the edge of the seat. Too easy. Try the same stunt while there's a guy in a suit still sitting on it. Now that's a challenge.

(You want to know how I did it? Nah, professional secret.)

My friends put me up to things and I fall for it every time. I just wish they'd hang around when things go wrong.

Things went wrong at Scream World not so long ago, and where were they? Nowhere to be seen. So there was me and a street sign I was busy relocating and three security guys who could have done a gorilla act in the circus—without costumes.

One of the security guards decided to make an example of me. He took me to the administration building and sat next to me while we waited to see the manager. I felt like I'd been sent to the principal's office at school. There was even a secretary typing and answering the phone. Just across from where I sat there was a door marked "G. K. WALTERS."

"You're in trouble, big time," said security. "Parents, police. Banned from Scream World for a hundred years. Maybe even community service."

He smiled to himself. No, he was grinning. Like this was a huge joke. The name on his shirt said "Fegan." No first name. With a face like that, his parents were probably too embarrassed to think of one.

"I'm only thirteen. They can't make you do community service if you're only thirteen."

"You're sure of that, are you?" said Fegan.

3

I wasn't, so I shut up.

From behind the manager's door I could hear shouting. Something about admission prices, I think. Then the door flew open and a man stormed out, with a face that said he'd just lost an argument. He wasn't much taller than me, or maybe losing an argument makes you look small. He disappeared into a room across the hall and slammed the door so hard the name plate almost fell off. "Ben Topler—Assistant Manager" it said.

Oh boy, my turn. Fegan shoved me through the door. "Prepare to meet your doom," he growled. I wasn't entirely convinced he was joking.

"What's your name?" asked the manager, who turns out to be a woman about Mom's age.

"Grommet."

"Your real name."

"Gromley."

"And do you have a first name?"

I do, but they'd have to torture me to make me say it.

I'd forgotten that Fegan went through my pockets when he nabbed me and found my wallet. "It's Charles, as in Prince." He laughed, and if I wasn't already in enough trouble I'd have kicked his fat butt.

"Well then, Max, what has Charles Gromley, nicknamed Grommet, been up to?"

"He was switching signs, making the Mountain of Terror sign point towards the Lethal Looper and vice versa," said Fegan.

"He's one of our saboteurs then?"

"Looks like it, Mrs. Walters. He'd already changed five other signs before we caught him."

Mrs. Walters narrowed her eyes and looked at me like I bite the heads off chickens for fun. "There's been too much of this lately. Sabotage, that's what it is. We're losing business. Last week someone locked all the stalls in the men's restrooms from the inside. We had a dozen poor fellows busting to go and all the time the stalls were empty. That sort of thing can give Scream World a bad reputation."

I tried to control the muscles at the corners of my mouth but it was no use. I kept seeing these men dancing from one leg to another and going red in the face. Mrs. Walters guessed what was going on.

"You did it! Look at his face, Max. He's smirking."

I had to nod because it was true. So now I'm in trouble for two crimes.

"You lit the fire in the ghost train as well, didn't you?"

"No, I'd never do that. That was dangerous. I saw it on the news. People could have been killed. I'd only ever do joke stuff, like those signs."

Max, the security man, didn't believe me but Mrs. Walters did. She told him to back off while she checked me over with her eyes. "How do you do it, Grommet? Max and his men have security cameras all over the park but you'd already changed five signs before he caught you."

"It's not so hard. I know where those cameras are. You can see them move. I just wait until they're pointing the other way. It's the same with the guys like him." I crooked my thumb and pointed towards Max Fegan, who was brewing up the dirtiest look I've ever seen on a human being. "They're easy to spot because of the uniforms."

Suddenly Max didn't look quite so angry. In fact, he was smirking. Why is that? I wondered. Then it hit me. "Of course, there are a few plain-clothes guys as well, but they all stand out like a pimple on the end of your nose. My friends and I play a game, picking them out. Too easy."

Max was back to hating me with a red-hot sizzle. "Will I call in the police now, Mrs. Walters?"

She had gone back to sit behind her desk. This time she was thinking hard and staring at me. "No, I have a better idea." She leaned forward, resting her elbows on the desk. "Grommet, how would you like to be an undercover agent?"

CHAPTER
2

"It's been happening for weeks now," said Mrs. Walters.

We were still in her office. In fact, she had invited me to sit in a comfortable chair while she explained. "First, a safety rail came loose on the Mountain of Terror. Then the refrigerator that holds all the ice cream was switched off overnight. Have you ever seen twelve hundred and fifty gallons of ice cream that you could row a boat in? Finally, there was the fire in the ghost train."

"Someone's out to make us look bad," said Max.

"Yes, and they are doing a good job. People read about the accidents in the newspaper and then they stay away, or go somewhere else to have a day out. I've been manager of Scream World for ten years. I love to see people having fun. I just had Ben Topler in here. He wants to increase our ticket prices. If we don't, he says we'll have to close down in a month."

"We'll find who's doing it, Mrs. Walters. We don't need any help from troublemakers like this young fool."

She held up her hand to make him stop. "You're doing your best, Max, I know. But I'm getting desperate. It's time to try something unusual. The boy's clever, he's got a sharp eye, and no one will suspect he's working for us."

"But he'll let you down. I was a policeman for twenty years before I started as a security guard. His sort always mess up."

"Well, if he does, you'll be there to catch him," she said.

Max looked like he couldn't wait. Seeing the grin of pleasure on his face, I know how a bowl of chips feels at a party. Life expectancy—zero.

"So it's agreed," said Mrs. Walters. "There are two weeks of vacation left before school starts again. You come in every day and look for suspicious characters or anyone up to no good. They won't notice you because you blend in so well with the crowds."

She looked at Max Fegan as she said this. The only crowd he could blend in with was a bunch of wrestlers from WWF.

Mrs. Walters fixed her eyes on me and suddenly she looked just as mean as Max. "If you don't cooperate, Charles Gromley, or if you get up to any mischief, I'll call in your parents, the police, the army, the air force, and anyone else who wants to squash a grommet."

I started the next day.

As we didn't have a clue who the enemy was, only Mrs. Walters and Max Fegan knew about me. That was good in some ways; in other ways not so good. It would have been cool to have a badge or something I could flash when I needed to go into a restricted area. I daydreamed about this. I saw myself walking up to a line of that yellow tape they use to mark off the scene of a crime. A policeman would try to stop me ducking under it and I'd get out this badge and say, "It's okay, I'm Special Agent Grommet. Now take me to the body."

But I had nothing like that and I had to buy my own lunch.

I started looking out for suspicious people. This was my first surprise. There were dozens, no, hundreds of suspicious-looking people all over Scream World.

One guy stood next to the same garbage can for forty minutes. I watched him. He had sunglasses and a hat down so low I couldn't see his face. He was wearing long socks with sandals. You can't get much weirder than that, if you ask me. He kept looking at his watch and getting more anxious and angry.

I was about to warn Max that this guy probably had a bomb in the garbage can when three kids came up to him and he suddenly turned into an ordinary father. He wasn't a very happy one either, judging by the talk he gave his kids.

This was bad enough, but the worst thing about looking for suspicious people was who looked *most* suspicious. It was kids like me! I spotted a bunch of five guys, fourteen years old maybe. They were giggling and shoving each other in the shoulder and checking around them every few seconds to see if anyone was watching.

They're planning something, I told myself. I followed them for an hour. They went on the Lethal Looper and the Gut Churner and shook up their Coke bottles so foamy-brown liquid sprayed everywhere when they opened them. They laughed so much at this, I thought they'd faint.

What was so funny? A bit of Coke gets wasted. It's not exactly sabotage!

But when the guys arrived at the Panther Prowl, I thought, this is it.

The panthers have their own enclosure with fences and a wide ditch keeping them in.

I expected the boys to chuck food over the ditch or shout wildly at the big cats to stir them up.

Nothing. They just kept looking around, as though they couldn't believe there were no teachers or parents to tell them to stand up straight, tuck their shirts in and generally behave themselves.

Freaks! If they'd put their caps round the right way, they wouldn't look like they were guilty of something.

CHAPTER

3

Since I was at the Panther Prowl, I thought I would take a closer look. It was just the kind of place to sabotage, after all. Imagine if those big cats got loose.

The enclosure had fences cleverly hidden in the bush at the sides, but, at the back, there was a high rock wall. A gate was set in this wall for the handlers to come and go. I followed the paths round behind the enclosure but, to get any closer, I had to walk down a lane for delivery trucks. At the end I found a door with "Staff Only" painted on it. Well, I was staff now so in I went.

There was nothing much to see, just one of those huge walk-in fridges like butchers have and another door, for the vet this time. I walked a bit further, then froze on the spot. One of the panthers had let rip with a roar that turned my guts to jelly. Luckily, it was a long way off from the enclosure on the far side of the wall.

I'd seen enough, though, and the prospect of meeting one of those panthers at close range had begun to worry me. I turned and headed back the way I had come. Five yards short of safety, a paw fell on my shoulder. Or at least I thought it was a paw. It was certainly heavy enough.

"What are you doing in here?"

This seemed like a fair question. I wasn't surprised to hear it. The surprise was the voice. It was hardly a human voice at all. It was like something from a bad sci-fi movie, one where the robots have taken over the planet and get nasty with human beings.

Whoever (or whatever) had hold of me, spun me around like a doll. It wasn't a robot. No, it was worse. The guy had a dark, sinister face and eyes that could punch holes like laser beams. Forget science fiction. This face had escaped from a horror movie.

He held on to me with that one hand. In the other, he was clutching something that looked like a small torch, though no light came out of the end. While I stood there terrified, he pressed it against his throat, next to the Adam's apple. It was only then that I saw the scar and realized that he didn't have an Adam's apple.

"You're here to disturb my animals," said that weird voice. His lips moved a little but the sound came from that thing in his hand.

"No, I just wanted to look around."

"You can see all you're supposed to see from the viewing area."

The voice sent shivers up my spine. "I'm sorry. I shouldn't be here, I know."

He grunted, through his mouth this time. I guess he didn't need any help to make that kind of noise. Another person turned up, a girl about twenty, in khaki shorts and shirt. He handed me over to her.

"Get him out of here."

The girl grabbed my arm and pushed me roughly towards the door.

"Okay, okay. I was snooping around where I shouldn't be."

"You're lucky," she said. "Trespassing like that. He might have knocked you out first and asked questions later. He has a bad temper sometimes."

I could believe it. "Who is he?"

"Mr. Larousse, the head keeper. He'll do any-thing to protect his panthers. You'd better not show your face in here again."

She kicked open the door and I was out in the sunlight again. She didn't exactly throw me on to the road but I certainly got the message.

"That voice of his?" I asked as she stood glaring at me to make sure I walked off up the lane. "And that thing he holds against his neck?"

"It's an amplifier. He had to learn to speak like that after the accident."

"Accident."

"A lion attacked him years ago. When a lion kills a zebra or a gazelle, it goes for the throat. Mr. Larousse was lucky. He pushed the lion off before it could kill him but it ripped all his vocal chords. Do you understand now? Mr. Larousse is not someone to tangle with."

CHAPTER

4

I couldn't get Mr. Larousse out of my mind. Everything about him dripped with evil. His frowning face, those eyes that burned my skin, the steely grip of his hand on my shoulder, and especially his voice. If anyone was cruel enough, mean enough, mad enough to sabotage Scream World it was him.

I decided to keep an eye on him. He stayed close by his panthers most of the next day until, finally, at lunchtime, I saw him slip out of the door marked "Staff Only." At the end of the lane, he looked one way carefully, then the other. Who is he trying to avoid? I wondered. Very suspicious.

I followed, keeping back so he wouldn't see me.

Wouldn't you know it? He must have spotted me anyway. One minute he was on his way towards the Lethal Looper and then he vanished. There were shops and ice-cream parlors on one side of the street but he wasn't in any of them.

I tried the other side of the street where a two-yard-high hedge fenced off the machinery for the ride. I hurried along this hedge, ducking low as I looked for a way through. There it was. A man wouldn't fit but I'm not as big. (My granddad says I'm thin as a whippet, whatever that is.)

Unfortunately, I made a bit of noise squeezing my way through. Well, actually, I swore like a trucker when a stiff branch tried to turn me into a shish kebab. But someone was there all right, Larousse most likely. All I saw was a shadow disappearing into the hedge further down. When I ran to check, I found a much bigger opening, though you would have to know it was there to find it. Whoever I'd seen knew this park very well.

But why was he here? I couldn't see anything damaged. There wasn't much to see, just some metal casings cemented into the ground and a power pole with one of those fuse boxes you see on the side of a house. The door swung loose in the breeze, flashing the name at me every few seconds: LETHAL LOOPER.

That was it! I raced to the pole and found a series of dials and switches. They were locked in place by a bar so that someone like me couldn't tamper with them but I was sure that they had been changed somehow.

Let's see, I said to myself. There were three sets of the same thing, two were switched on, the third switched off. There was something odd about the last switch. At its base, the plastic was shiny because there was no dust on it.

I looked up at the ride. It's your average roller coaster, starting off at the ground, climbing slowly and becoming very, very high until the train shoots down the other side and then through one loop, a second loop, and finally . . .

I was already running. The roller coaster train was filling up quickly and any minute it would set off. There wasn't a long wait so no one shouted at me for jumping the line. The attendant was a man with a ponytail and goateed beard.

"You can't let this ride go," I shouted.

"What!"

"It's too dangerous. There's going to be an accident."

He stayed calm. "There's no need to panic, man. It'll be all right. Lots of people are scared the first time."

"No, you don't understand. People might get killed."

"No, it's perfectly safe. Ridden in it a hundred times myself. It's fun." He started to lead me towards the carriage.

"No." I pulled away. "Get them all out. Close down the ride."

"Now, look, just because you're scared doesn't mean other people can't have fun."

By this time, two boys had come up the ramp. "What's his problem? Lost his nerve, has he? Afraid of heights. You'd better let the coward go home to his mommy."

Now, no one tells me to run home to Mommy and I didn't like being called a coward, either. What happened next is a bit hazy but I do know one thing for certain. Thirty seconds later, that train did set off on the roller coaster ride—and I was sitting in the last row of seats.

CHAPTER

5

My first thought was, who will come to my funeral? Would Max Fegan, the security man, show up? Mrs. Walters, the manager, would send flowers, maybe. That would be good of her. I hope it was a nice funeral.

Then I felt the safety bar in front of me, padded so people didn't hurt themselves as they rattled around at a million miles an hour. Most of all, the safety bar was to stop passengers from falling out when the train went upside down through the loops. A science teacher tried to tell us that we wouldn't fall out even if there was no bar. Something called centrifugal force would keep us stuck in our seats.

After what was about to happen to everyone on that roller coaster, I'm going back to see that teacher and tell him what he can do with his centrifugal force.

There were the usual screams when we started down the steep slope. Before I could blink, we were into the first loop with the whole world upside down. Then it was right side up for a second, then upside down again. Go for it, I thought, third loop here we come. We swooped into it, the world flipped on its lid and then we stopped.

Roller coasters aren't supposed to stop, at least not until they arrive back where they started from. We ended up at the top of the third loop, stationary and silent, and a long way from the ground.

Did I say the ride was silent? The silence lasted

about five seconds, until the passengers realized this wasn't how it was supposed to be. Women screamed, men shouted in terror, girls became frantic and boys went hysterical, even the under-cover agent, who still couldn't work out why he was here when he knew something like this was going to happen.

"Don't panic, don't panic," a man shouted. He was sitting (well, hanging) four seats in front of me. He managed to stop a few of the screamers and the others toned it down a little. "We'll be okay. The cars can't fall from these rails. We just have to wait until they rescue us. Don't do any-thing silly and we'll all walk away alive."

He obviously knew more than my science teacher and it looked for a while like everyone believed him. Then a boy in front of me, one of the pair who had called me a coward, started up again. "I can't stand it. We're too far up. I've got to get down, I've got to get down."

He started to push at his safety bar.

"No," shouted the man who had calmed us all. "Stay where you are. It's your best chance."

The boy wasn't listening. The safety bar was locked in place, but he was a weedy kid like me and I could see he was wriggling his way free.

"You'll fall," I told him.

"Shut up!"

Once he was free of that safety bar, he was dead meat.

"Hey, what are you doing?" cried the girl in the next seat when she saw me squeezing round the end of my own safety bar. "You'll both be killed."

Good point.

"Look. There's a truck coming." She pointed towards it, which is hard to do when the whole world is upside down. I had seen this kind of truck before. They're called cherry-pickers, though I've

29

only ever seen council workers use them to reach the top of power poles. No cherries up there. All we had to do was wait and we would be picked off like, well, cherries.

Tell that to the maniac who was still struggling to get free. The truck was closer now but it wouldn't get here in time. I had to do something. The girl's words rang in my ears. *You'll both be killed.* I looked at her and noticed something I don't usually notice about girls—what she was wearing. Starting at the bottom, she had long blonde hair, earrings that dangled the wrong way, a white top with narrow shoulder straps and, on top, jeans and a pink belt. I even asked to borrow a part of her clothing and I've certainly never done that before.

By the time I strained and pulled my way free of the safety bar, the frantic boy in front had squeezed his own way out. As soon as he was free, he fell.

I just had time to lunge forward and grab him

in the best tackle I have ever done in my life. I wish my football coach was there to see it.

Now, with both my arms locked round the boy, I couldn't hold on to anything myself. Gravity should have made us both plummet straight down to the ground.

There was no plummeting. I'd taken precautions, hadn't I? It was like that old song we sang in preschool. My arms were connected to my body, my body to my legs, my legs to my ankles, and my ankles weren't going anywhere. I'd tied them tightly to the safety bar with the girl's belt.

It was a strong-looking belt, about two inches wide, and leather too. Mom was always going on about how strong leather was and not to use plastics and other junk. Always go for the genuine article, she said.

It wasn't the belt I worried about up there, sixty feet above the ground. It was my arms. They were

31

killing me. The panicky boy might have looked skinny but he weighed a ton. One of my hands was locked over my other wrist to hold on to his body, but we were both sweating badly and I could feel my grip slipping. Where was that crane?

"Don't drop me. Don't drop me," he pleaded.

I dropped him. Or at least my arms burst apart and he began to fall. My hands have never moved so fast in my life. Just as it seemed I'd lost him, each of my hands managed to grab a fistful of his T-shirt.

Unfortunately, T-shirts aren't made for holding up a human body. They're for slipping on and off easily. The boy was slipping out of his all too easily.

"Help me!" he shouted desperately.

But I couldn't do anything except hold on to that stretched and straining material. With a final scream, he was gone, leaving me with just an empty T-shirt dangling in mid-air.

CHAPTER

6

Don't panic. He hadn't gone far. In fact, if he had
wanted to, he could have reached up and taken
his T-shirt out of my hand because the cherry-
picker had arrived just in time.

Just in time for me too! All that weight had
been too much for the girl's belt. Leather or no
leather, it snapped and, without warning, I fell
head-first into the fiberglass bucket. Luckily, my
fall was broken by the body of the boy who was
curled up in a whimpering ball on the floor.

The bucket was quickly lowered to ground

level so we could stagger out. Some people kiss the ground after they have a scare like that. I wanted to hug it tenderly and discuss a long-term relationship.

The bucket didn't stay down for long. A man in orange overalls with "EMERGENCY" sewn across the back jumped in, and off he went to rescue the other passengers.

"You were amazing, a hero, you saved this boy's life," a man said.

The other boy was led away shaking but I had to stay while this man told me how absolutely fantastic I was. I could handle that. Normally people tell me how awful I am.

But I knew this guy. He was the one who'd stormed out of the manager's office while I was waiting to go in. He had been too angry that day to see anyone else so I was certain he didn't recognize me.

"My name's Ben Topler," he said, shaking my hand. "I'm the Assistant Manager of Scream World. Saw the whole thing. You were very brave to get out of your seat like that."

I tried to look embarrassed. "I was terrified. And we were lucky that crane turned up so quickly," I said, trying to sound less like a hero.

By now, others were crowding round. "What happened. Why did the ride stop like that?"

"It's like we're jinxed," Mr. Topler told them.

"Doesn't seem very safe," said a woman with two kids at her side.

"We're doing our best," he assured her, but she wasn't convinced and I saw her lead her family towards the exit.

Mr. Topler turned back to me. "Now, young man. You are the hero of the hour. The television people will want to interview you and the news-papers. Your face will be all over the place, a household name. You'll be famous."

There was a commotion as two crying girls were reunited with their mother. This gave me a moment to think. Famous, a hero, my name in the newspapers, and my face on TV. Mom and Dad would want to know what I was doing at Scream World when I'd told them I was going to Josh Carter's place.

Worst of all, my cover would be blown. I couldn't sneak around Scream World, looking for saboteurs unnoticed if every ten yards someone pointed a finger at me and said, "Hey, there's that boy hero." I might as well wear a Superman suit.

I still wanted to help Mrs. Walters. I liked her. I liked the way she spoke about Scream World. It meant a lot to her. This was a challenge and, as I've said already, I'm a sucker for a challenge. While Ben Topler turned away to sympathize with the girls and their mother, I slipped quietly into the crowd. I had a suspect for the Lethal Looper accident. It was time I let Max Fegan know about it, so a few hours later when the commotion had died down, I climbed the stairs that led to the security office. A guy even uglier than Max opened the door. "You must be lost, friend. There's no rides up here."

"I have to speak to Mr. Fegan."

"Yeah. And why would he want to speak to you?"

If I had my undercover agent's badge, I could flash it and this man would suddenly grovel at my feet in apology. That was a fantasy though, I reminded myself. "He's my Uncle Max," I lied. It was enough to get me inside.

The place was amazing. There were a couple of tiny offices but the first thing that caught my eye was a storeroom with the door open. Inside, there were chains and handcuffs and canisters of tear gas, riot shields and helmets. Security guards must have a lot of fun.

But I soon forgot all about that storeroom when I saw the television monitors. There were seven of them in a long row and in front of them was a console with dials and knobs and switches. Max Fegan sat before this console, stabbing at buttons with his left hand while he moved a joystick around with his right. He could see every bit of Scream World through those monitors. I was never going to be happy with an ordinary video game after this.

I guess my face showed my excitement and it was this excitement that worried Max. He still thought of me as "the enemy" and he didn't think it was such a good idea to show the enemy his best weapon.

"What'd you bring him in here for?"

"He said you're his uncle."

"*Uncle!*" Max shoved me away from the console into his office.

"I know what happened to the Lethal Looper," I told him.

He didn't believe me, but when I insisted, he came with me to look at the fuse box. There were the three switches, each locked into position by the bar just as before, except that these weren't the way I had seen them only a couple of hours ago. The third switch was turned on now, the same as the first two.

"But he tampered with it. I'm certain."

"Who tampered with it?"

"The lion tamer," I said in a hurry.

It shouldn't have surprised me when Max looked a bit confused. Obviously, I was confused myself.

"I mean the guy who takes care of the panthers."

"Ted Larousse! You've got to be joking." He grabbed me by the front of my shirt. The high hedge kept us hidden from view so he could threaten me all he liked. "Now tell me the truth, you little bag of bones. Did you actually see him, with your own eyes? Did you see him standing at this box, tampering with the switches?"

Well, actually, I hadn't. I had followed him from the Panther Prowl. I'd lost him. I had seen a figure disappearing through the hedge but I couldn't say who it was.

I admitted all this to Max Fegan and he let me go.

"That's better. If you want me to take you seriously, then find some evidence."

I wasn't going to give up on Mr. Larousse, though, and later that day I found out something that made me all the more suspicious.

Mrs. Walters had been to inspect the Lethal

Looper. On the way back to her office, she spotted me and called me over. "How are things going? Do you know anything about today's accident?"

I shook my head but she gave me five dollars to pig-out with anyway. Out of curiosity, I asked her about Mr. Larousse.

"He's very good with the big cats but he keeps to himself most of the time, poor man. I don't know him very well. You'd do better to ask Max Fegan. He and Ted Larousse are great friends."

CHAPTER 7

What is the greatest danger to the undercover agent? Guns, knives, bombs? For James Bond those might be a problem but I haven't seen any of those around Scream World. Some spies might give themselves away by saying too much and, of course, you could always be double-crossed by someone who knew you were an undercover agent—someone like Max Fegan.

But I found out the greatest danger is your friends. They know your face, they can pick you out in a crowd, draw attention to you because they don't know how important it is to go unnoticed.

My friends turned up on the third day. I was hanging around the Panther Prowl, watching for Mr. Larousse, and because I'm not very good at this job yet, I wasn't watching for anyone else.

"Grommet!" It was Josh Carter.

I spun round quickly and there was Ganger Williams and Dave Beck. There was a fourth kid with them but I hadn't seen him before.

"We didn't know you were coming here today," Josh continued. He had the loudest voice. It felt like the entire world had turned to look at us.

"Who's this?" I asked, nodding towards the new boy.

"Toby. Great name, isn't it? With a name like that, we had to beat him up or let him join, didn't we, Tobes?"

Toby looked more in favor of the second option.

"He's on probation," said Ganger.

I knew what that meant. Trouble for me. "It's time Toby proved himself, eh, guys? This'll be a good start." He kicked violently at a vending machine beside him. "Maybe we'll get Tobes to break it open for us," and he gave the machine another kick with his size-eight Nikes.

Not now, guys, I thought to myself. I'm busy. I glanced around and, sure enough, half a dozen faces had turned to look at us. On top of that, one of the security cameras was pointing straight at us. Josh and the boys could wave hello to Max Fegan if they wanted to. It was just what he needed to make me look bad in front of Mrs. Walters. He was probably recording this whole meeting.

"Come on, Grommet. You might as well hang with us now."

I wasn't going to see much around the Panther

Prowl with this cheer squad making everyone stare at us. And it would look suspicious if I didn't join them.

After five minutes of walking, we reached the center of Scream World, a big square of grass with fountains and ponds and park benches where families came to eat their lunch. Here Josh spotted a way to initiate poor Toby.

"You see that woman over there, the one with three little kids. She's left her handbag on the baby stroller while she feeds them. Steal it."

Toby looked like he'd rather wrestle an anaconda.

"Don't do it," I said to Toby.

"What's the matter with you, Grommet?" said Josh. Ganger and Dave looked just as surprised. "You're going soft," said Ganger.

I should have told them all about the cameras. There were two in this area of the park and both

45

of them were looking on our little group. But if I told them that, it was like giving away secrets.

I stayed where I was, but Josh, Ganger, and Dave made it easier for their new recruit. They moved off a little way and started to toss an empty Coke bottle around in a game of touch football. It worked. The woman kept an eye on them in case their boisterous game came too close to her children. Toby was in like a flash and took the handbag.

Oh, great. He should have smiled for the cameras. Me too for that matter because I was dressed the same as them, and I was hanging around with them. It would look like I was part of it. Max had me on toast. I knew he would be on his way here right now, to nab me in person.

The other three had joined Toby by now, hurrying down one of the wide streets that led away from the square. I ran after them and snatched back the handbag.

"What are you doing, Gromley?" Ganger snapped angrily.

"Yeah, give it back." Josh was standing shoulder to shoulder with Dave, but I didn't hang around waiting for them to start a fight. They followed as I headed back the way we'd come and by then they could guess where I was going. This made them stop in their tracks. Up ahead, I could see the lady and her kids. She had just realized her handbag was missing but she couldn't race off looking for it and leave those three alone.

"Excuse me, excuse me," I called. When I was only a yard or two away, I stopped. "You dropped this, I think."

She came forward and took it from my outstretched hand, then stepped back quickly. "How did you know it was mine?"

Good point.

"Er . . . I . . . er, I saw it fall off your baby stroller."

"But I've been here for ten minutes. Why did it take you so long?"

Come on, lady, I thought. Just be grateful you've got your handbag back.

She opened it and quickly found her purse. The notes and coins were all there so she relaxed a little. "I suppose I should thank you," she said but she didn't.

I walked off before she asked me any more questions I couldn't answer. If I avoided my friends, they would only follow me so I walked straight at them. With the woman still watching, they fell into step with me until we were round a corner. "Have you turned into a goody-two-shoes now?" said Josh, with a sneer. "Why'd you have to give the handbag back like that? We weren't really going to steal anything from it. It was just a test for Toby."

It went on like that for about a minute with Dave and Ganger having a go at me as well. They made it pretty clear I was out of the group.

I was upset. These guys were my friends. We tortured teachers together, we played handball every lunch hour and then we went home to each other's fridges. Who was I going to mess around with now?

When Josh and the rest were finished unloading their disgust, they took off. It wouldn't be so easy for me. I looked around and, yes, there was Max Fegan, waiting for me, just as I knew he would be. I felt like holding out my hands for the handcuffs like they do on TV.

"I was watching," he said.

"Yeah, I know, the cameras."

"I saw what you did."

I shrugged. If he wanted to say I'd stolen the handbag in the first place, I wasn't going to squeal.

Mrs. Walters wouldn't believe me anyway.

"I heard what your friends said to you as well. Pretty rough." He certainly didn't look like he was about to arrest me. "Maybe you're not the kid I thought you were. I know how it feels to have friends like that, you know."

I must have looked at him surprised. "Oh, I was a cop once, sure, but before that I wasn't exactly an altar boy. I know guts when I see it. Come on, we've both got work to do. There's a guy somewhere here trying to sabotage the place and we have to find him."

CHAPTER
8

I wasn't quite sure whether it was easier having Max Fegan as an enemy or a friend. He was a sort of suspect, after all, because he was close friends with Mr. Larousse.

Could I trust him? This is the big question that undercover agents ask all the time. I have seen enough movies to know that if they get the answer wrong, they can end up as roadkill.

The days passed. I discovered that Mr. Larousse ate a hamburger for lunch every day, the same type, bought at the same place at the same time. He drove a genuine, bone-rattling Land Rover, not one of those pampered four-wheel drives with stereo CD players and air conditioning. Wherever he went, he left an odor, a mixture of straw and animal fur and the odd whiff of something more earthy.

But I still couldn't find the evidence that showed he was the saboteur. At least there were no more accidents.

Then disaster. It wasn't sabotage, not the type I was hunting for, and it didn't even happen inside the park. No, it began in my own home. I came home, exhausted after a whole day on the knife-edge as an undercover agent, and as I stepped through the front door, my little brother tackled me. Brett is only seven and usually when he tries to tackle me, he bounces off. This time I ended up on my face, eating carpet.

"We're going to Scream World," he shouted in my ear.

"Who?"

"Tessa and me. Mom and Dad are taking us."

Tessa is ten and doesn't play football. However, she certainly knows how to jump on top of a tackle. "It's because we've been good all summer," she said from the end of the hall.

The message was obvious. I hadn't managed to be good all summer so I wasn't invited. In fact, I was banned from having fun for the rest of my life.

Mom appeared in the doorway behind Tessa. She looked a little guilty but it was true.

"But you can't go to Scream World," I yelled at them.

This was the last thing I needed. Undercover agents are useless once their cover is blown. Unfortunately, my parents thought I had other motives for objecting.

"It serves you right," said Mom. "Let this be a lesson to you."

"No, you don't understand." I was desperate and began clutching at any excuse I could think of. "It's . . . it's too expensive."

"Not tomorrow. Look, it's free." Dad held up the newspaper, showing a large advertisement. *Open Day at Scream World.*

I had heard Mrs. Walters and Ben Topler arguing about this. Ben was against the idea. A waste of money, he called it. They had lost enough already since the accidents started.

Mrs. Walters had insisted. They needed people to come and see how much fun it all was and how safe. She had invited the television stations to come along and film the crowds.

I argued with my parents even harder than Ben Topler had argued with Mrs. Walters. Both of us lost. "It's just sour grapes," my father told me.

Tessa poked her tongue out at me. Brett looked like he would tackle me again so I told him what

I'd do if he tried.

He didn't.

I lay awake all night wondering how I was going to avoid them and still do my job. Nothing cropped up to let me sleep easily.

Then, three minutes after I walked into Scream World, I found the answer, or at least it found me. I was watching for my parents when a large furry thing bumped into me.

"Oh, sorry," said a kangaroo.

I'm not crazy. I know kangaroos can't talk. This was a life-sized character from the cartoons on television. The head came off the body and I found myself staring at a boy about sixteen. "Phew. It's so hot in here. I'm going to die."

It took about three minutes to convince him to let me take his place. "What are you going to do in this thing, anyway?" he wanted to know.

"Play tricks on my friends. Come on, you're melting. If you let me switch with you, you can have fun all day and still get paid at the end for being a kangaroo."

"Not unless I'm wearing that suit at five o'clock," he said and I knew from the look on his face that he was seriously thinking about it.

"All right, all right. I'll meet you back here at half-past four."

He was sold.

Now I was a kangaroo and a very hot one at that. After half an hour I was beginning to understand what a lobster feels like when it's dropped into hot water. I ripped a hole in the seams under each armpit for a bit of cross-ventilation and that brought the temperature down a few degrees.

The shade of the fake rainforest was very inviting but I had to move around to have any chance of stopping the sabotage. There were some definite benefits to being a furry animal as well. A Japanese woman gave me the biggest hug and for a moment I thought I would get the same from three absolute babes. Instead, they took turns standing beside me while the third one snapped a photo.

Perhaps this was a sign that my luck was turning south. The bulky suit made me awkward when people crowded round and, to make matters worse, it had a joey in its pouch. I knocked over three little kids and a grandma before I learned not to turn round suddenly. Then a cute little girl tried to tug the poor joey right out of its pouch.

"Help! Someone's trying to take my baby," I shouted. It was just a joke. A real kangaroo would have given her a good kick but the girl started to cry and her mother told me off. This day wasn't going well.

And, before much longer, it was going to get a lot worse.

CHAPTER

I wondered whether I should let Max know I was in disguise. He had been good to me after my friends had stolen the handbag. In the last few days we had developed respect for each other. I might even admit that I liked him, though not to his face. Then, yesterday, when I followed Mr. Larousse on his lunch break, who should turn up to have a burger with him but Max Fegan.

They sat together for twenty minutes, deep in serious discussion. I could just hear the robot sounds coming from the little amplifier. "Mountain" was definitely one of the words. That could only mean the Mountain of Terror, but were they talking about the safety rail from two weeks ago or what they intended to do next? It was Max himself who had told me the importance of solid evidence and not just suspicions.

A good undercover agent has to be daring but also cautious. I wouldn't tell Max just yet.

But if no one knew I had been a kangaroo all day, Mrs. Walters might think I had cheated on our deal and gone surfing instead.

So I went to see her.

"I'm sorry. Mrs. Walters is in a meeting right now."

"It's important."

"So is this meeting. The owners have come to see her. I can hardly barge in and say there's a kangaroo waiting to see her, can I?"

Good point.

I put my head back on and walked out into the sunshine. Just as well my face was hidden because Ben Topler, the Assistant Manager, was hurrying up the stairs. If he had recognized me from the Lethal Looper, I would have had to explain my special role as an undercover agent.

My kangaroo suit wasn't made for easy walking. Even old grannies with walkers raced past me like I was standing still. At least I had plenty of time to observe the crowd. To my surprise, Ben Topler passed me again, going in the same direction this time and sticking to the edge of the wide streets where he could move faster. I knew the park like the back of my furry paw by now and I guessed he was heading for the Panther Prowl. Mrs. Walters had persuaded not just one but three television stations to send their cameras along. I'd seen tripods and microphones being set up earlier and Ben Topler had been buzzing around asking if they needed anything. "Keep your eyes on those panthers," he'd insisted.

It's a strange thing about television cameras. Set one up and people will come from all around, expecting something exciting to happen. A large crowd had gathered, including Mom and Dad and Tessa and Brett.

I was so busy avoiding them that I almost bumped into Topler. This time, he hadn't joined the cameramen and the pretty reporter with the microphone in her hand. He had stopped near the lane that led to the back of the enclosure and was looking at something some distance away, something high off the ground.

I turned to see what it was but at first I was baffled. No birds, no low-flying planes, just a pole with one of Max's cameras on top. While I was watching the camera, it moved to a new position. When I turned back to where Topler was standing, he was gone.

It took a moment to find him. He had slipped down the service road towards the rear of the enclosure. He's going to see Mr. Larousse, I decided. On a day like today, it was important to have the panthers looking good and doing whatever panthers do.

Well, that wasn't my job. Time to get back to the world of an undercover agent. I took a step backwards, but, for some reason, my eye stayed on Topler as he hurried down the tree-lined lane. What I saw in the next few seconds changed everything. He was about to open the "Staff Only" door when he sprang back suddenly, looked around frantically, then ducked behind a row of wheel bins.

Moments later, the door opened and Mr. Larousse marched out. He didn't notice Topler behind the bins. In twenty purposeful strides, he reached the corner where I stood. Of course, Larousse didn't know it was me but he still managed to glare at the outfit with a look that said, "What a fool. Who would walk around dressed like a silly kangaroo for a living?"

I didn't have time to see where Larousse went after that. Suddenly it had become more important to watch Topler, who, glancing over his shoulder, pushed his way carefully inside the Panther Prowl.

CHAPTER
10

Should I follow Topler or not? Oh, what the heck! I've been banned from plenty of places and it hasn't stopped me yet.

The only problem was getting through the doorway. My big-butted roo was too wide, so it was time to become just plain Grommet again. The cool air of the darkened space chilled the perspiration that had already soaked my shirt. Family or no family, I wasn't getting back into that outfit again.

Where was Topler? I crept forward, staying in

the shadows close to the walls. There was someone ahead but I couldn't tell whether it was him or
not. At last the figure came towards me, into the
brightness under a skylight, and I saw it was the
woman who told me about Larousse and the lion.

Her mind was on her job, not intruders. She
turned into the storeroom I had seen on my earlier visit. No sooner did she step inside, than
someone sprang out of the darkness and slammed
the door behind her. Before she knew what had
happened, he'd locked the door and shoved the
key into his pocket.

She banged against it with her fists and shouted
but no one could hear her. No one but me.

What type of sabotage did Topler have in mind
this time?

I tracked his movements through the shadows
until I heard the large refrigerator open and close.
Under the skylight I caught a glimpse of what he

held in his hands. Meat. Five, six large hunks of it. He dropped one hunk at his feet and threw two back towards the gates that led into the enclosure. The rest he used to make a trail all the way to the door that led out into the lane. Then he pulled the door open and jammed a piece of wood in place to keep the door open.

What should I do? Without a key, I couldn't get the woman out of the storeroom. As soon as he moved back towards the gates, I could run for help. But I wasn't sure where Max was. Even if he was in his office, that was on the other side of Scream World. Through a crowd like today's, it would take seven, maybe ten minutes to reach him and another ten to run back. By then, Topler would have released the panthers.

Someone could get hurt. My family was out there. It might be one of them! What could Max and his men do anyway? They would have to shoot the panthers. Mrs. Walters, Mr. Larousse, even Max himself, would lose their jobs.

Topler had gone towards the gates into the enclosure. I hurried to the door he had propped open and kicked away the piece of wood.

Idiot! Why didn't I pull it away slowly with my hand? The wood scraped loudly across the concrete, surprising me, and in that instant I let go of the door. If the original noise wasn't enough to alert Topler, the sound of that door slamming certainly was.

"Who's there?" he hissed. I tried to hide but in a matter of seconds he'd found me. He lunged at me but I'm a weed, remember, a whippet, and I slipped under his arm.

Unfortunately, he was between me and the door, so true escape wasn't an option just yet. In fact, there wasn't much space to get around in and I wasn't eager to go too close to the gate of the enclosure. Once he grabbed me, I didn't stand a chance. He was much stronger than me. I needed something to even up the score, a weapon of some kind, but the best I could find was a broom. When he came at me, I shoved the coarse bristles in his face.

This was enough to make Topler back away but then it was his turn to hunt for weapons and, unlike mine, his luck was in. He reached up and took a rifle from a special harness on the wall. In the dim light, that was all I could see. He raised it to his shoulder, his finger on the trigger. This was going to be my last moment alive on Planet Earth and when that happens, you say some strange things like, "Hey, I'm only thirteen. You can't kill me like this. I'd rather do community service."

Maybe I fainted for a second or two, maybe I tried to jump away at the last minute. *Thwack!* Something hit the wall beside my shoulder. A dart. This gun shot only tranquilizing darts and not very accurately, it seemed. He was loading another dart into the rifle. *Time to go.*

I couldn't get past him. I would have to go over him. To my right, the wall was made of massive boulders, part of the enclosure itself. I climbed as quickly as I could, just getting high enough before Topler's grasping hand snatched at my heels.

He went back to loading the gun. I kept climbing. Right now, my skinny little bottom was making the perfect target. My arms ached, my feet struggled to find a foothold. I don't know how I did it but suddenly I was on top of the wall. Sunlight beat down on me as though I had stepped into the spotlight on a stage.

Where was I? What was on the other side of this rock wall? A noise reached my ears and suddenly I knew, without needing to look down. Panthers. One, two, no . . . three, and that one in the shadows makes four. I lost count after that.

I turned back, looking down towards Topler. He had the gun raised to his shoulder again. My next movement was all instinct. After all, who would just stand there and let a guy shoot a tranquilizer dart into his leg or stomach?

I jumped out of the way, didn't I? The only trouble was that there was only one way to jump.

CHAPTER
11

As falls go, I've had worse. No bones were broken and the only blood on show came from the grazes on my palms. But I had more to worry about than the dull pain in my hands.

It was a spectacular entrance, I have to admit, and the panthers weren't likely to miss it. They simply stared at me at first as though I had dropped in for lunch unexpectedly. Maybe I had!

This gave me a minute to look around. Whoever built the enormous rock wall behind me had made sure that from this side, no one, man or beast, was going to climb it. It was a cliff face, with no spaces for hands or feet or paws to get a hold. Scratch one method of escape.

On my left was the wide ditch that separated the enclosure from the gaping crowd. There was a lot of extra gaping going on right now. I wished I was with them, watching some other poor fool get torn apart by panthers.

At least my death would be recorded on film, a sort of action-replay for my family. There they were, Mom and Dad, looking as stunned as the rest, though Tessa and Brett were probably saying I'd planned this to embarrass them. I didn't think it was the moment to wave.

One of the panthers started towards me, slowly, with real stealth, like I was an antelope caught alone on the African plains. I'll never watch another wildlife program again.

A second and then a third big cat decided to

take a look. Before I knew it, I had five panthers closing in, all timing their movement to arrive at the same time. Maybe it's bad manners among panthers to start eating before everyone else.

I felt the wall hard against my back. Across the ditch, a horrified scream rang out, "Help him, someone," but the ditch kept people out as well as panthers in. Not even an Olympic long jumper could get across. I thought about my funeral again and wondered if there would be anything left to bury.

"Don't move," said a familiar voice, although it wasn't a voice I was fond of. The robot squawk of Mr. Larousse was talking to me. "Whatever you do, don't run. They'll know you are prey then and they'll rip your throat out in seconds."

Where was he? I dared a glance towards the ditch. No sign of him. I checked the other way and there he was, in the enclosure with me, one hand holding his amplifier in place, the other hand gripped round the handle of a whip. "Stay where you are. I'll drive them off."

He edged his way cautiously across the grass in a wide half-circle until he was between me and the panthers. The first crack of the whip made me jump more than the big cats. At least he had their attention and that meant they might forget about me. This was no time for heroic plans of my own. He'd told me to stay where I was and that's what I did.

Slowly he began to force them back but they were spread widely in front of him and as soon as he advanced on one side, the others would try to slip round him and he had to turn quickly, lashing at them. They hissed and growled at him, turning my guts to marshmallow, but they were afraid of that whip and Mr. Larousse's harsh mechanical voice.

It was working. Step by step, yard by yard, he made them retreat, even the biggest one on his right, which gave out a frightening, high-pitched snarl every time he cracked the whip. Further, further. I think I managed to breathe again about then. They were twenty yards away, twenty-five. Phew! I wasn't going to be Grommet steak after all.

At that moment, a second keeper rushed into the enclosure. I'm sure it was a very brave thing to do and all he wanted was to rescue me, but I wish he'd left all that to Mr. Larousse. The clang of the gate opening and closing distracted the panthers. They forgot the whip and ran off in every direction, most of them as far away from me as possible. I was pleased about that.

Unfortunately, one of them started back towards me, the big one, the noisy one. Just my luck, he was probably the hungriest. Was it any less painful to be mauled by one panther than five?

"Grommet, Grommet." This was no metal voice from a machine. It was a commanding male voice, strong but with a touch of anxious concern about it. It was just how I imagined God's voice would be.

It was coming from above me. Oh no. What next! Would my whole life flash before my eyes? As the huge black beast munched through my body, was my soul going to float up and away to join that voice?

"Grommet, here, grab this."

Something touched my head, then dangled before my eyes. A rope! And that voice. Max!

Looking up, I found him on top of the wall in exactly the spot where I had stood before I jumped. "Grab the rope," he said again.

My hands were a mess of scratches that stung like fire when I took hold. How could I climb to safety?

One look at the advancing panther changed my mind. I planted my foot against the rock wall and started hand over hand. After a few moments, I was horizontal but it was hard work and much, much too slow. The cat was almost on me.

Thump. The rope was tugged hard from above me and I lost my footing on the rocks.

Fear saved me. It locked my hands around that rope as Max hauled with all his wrestler's strength. I felt myself rising quickly, my feet dangling free.

How high was I? More importantly, was I high enough? I looked down and that was a very silly thing to do. Much too close below me was that huge panther. I was certain it had doubled in size in the last ten seconds. It leapt up at me and only missed taking off my leg at the knee because I jerked sideways.

"Hurry, Max!"

He was pulling with all his might and up I went, two quick tugs, maybe a yard closer to the top. The panther sprang after me again and I felt a sharp pain on the sole of my foot but Max kept pulling and before it could have another go, I was too high for it to reach me. As long as I didn't slip back, anyway.

Poor Max, he was grunting and swearing but he wouldn't let go.

Three feet. Two. One . . . And then I could get my arm over the top of the wall, safe at last.

I sat up and pulled off my shoe. There was a thin line of blood tingeing the grubby white of my socks. When I looked at the shoe, there was a neat slash through the rubber sole, three inches long.

CHAPTER
12

When I explained what had happened, Max handed Ben Topler over to the police. Later Topler confessed to causing all the accidents—the fire in the Ghost Train, the safety rail on the Mountain of Terror, and it was him I'd seen disappearing through the hedge near the Lethal Looper.

"Why?" they asked him.

Wouldn't you know it. He was a kind of under-cover agent himself except that he was working *against* Scream World. Some shady business types had offered him a bunch of cash to make the place look bad. Once it was closed down, these crooks were going to buy the land, build luxury houses on it, and sell them off for a squillion bucks. How warped is that? If you ask me, the world doesn't need any more luxury houses, it needs more fun places like Scream World.

Of course, before I found all this out, I had to face the television cameras. I wasn't the hero this time. That honor belonged to Max and Mr. Larousse who had rescued me, especially Mr. Larousse who had run out into the enclosure and driven off most of the panthers.

"What happened?" the pretty reporter asked breathlessly. "Was this another accident?"

I was all set to tell the truth, but when she asked this question, I hesitated. If I told them that the assistant manager had tried to let the panthers loose, Scream World would be done for. No one would dare come here any more.

"It was a stunt," I said.

No one looked more surprised than Mrs. Walters, who was standing close by.

I winked at Max, who was clever for a security guard. He knew what I was doing. "Yes, we wanted to put on a show for you all, didn't we, Ted?"

Mr. Larousse was a shy man and he didn't want to use his amplifier in front of the camera. He just nodded.

"Well, we were certainly fooled," said the reporter, smiling now to show her brilliant white teeth.

Hundreds of people were gathered round. They started to clap. They were still clapping when my family pushed their way through the crowd. Mom and Dad didn't quite know what to say. Mrs. Walters was smiling and saying what a great guy I was. Max had his hand on my shoulder like I was his best friend. Even Mr. Larousse had a crooked smile on his crooked lips.

We had found the saboteur and, with my face about to go out on every television station in the country, my life as an undercover agent was well and truly over. I would have to go back to being a thirteen-year-old skater.

I wasn't sure that was going to be as much fun as it had been before. After all, my friends had turned against me and, come to think of it, I didn't really want them as friends any more. From now on, being Grommet would have to be more than just wearing my cap backwards and pulling crazy moves on my skateboard. I felt a bit uneasy about that.

Then, "Excuse me," said a voice.

I turned round to see a man with tanned skin, gangster sunglasses, and a heavy gold chain around his neck. He came closer and took off his glasses. "I make movies in a studio not far from here. I've got a job for you, if you're interested."

A job. What sort of job? No more undercover agent, and I certainly wasn't going to wear a kangaroo suit ever again.

My imagination kicked in. He wants me to be a movie star, I thought. My face would be on the cover of a hundred magazines and I'd have a limousine all to myself.

"After what I have just seen, you would be perfect," he said.

What did that mean? I had just been saved from man-eating panthers. "Exactly what job did you have in mind?"

"You'll love it," he said smiling. "What I need is a stuntman."

About James Moloney

James Moloney was born in Sydney in 1954, which makes him pretty old. He lives in Brisbane these days with his long-suffering wife and three children. They think he's "orright" and one of them lists him as her third-favorite author.

He was a teacher-librarian for twenty years, but he now writes novels for children and young adults. He's not bad either. Many of his books have won awards, including *A Bridge to Wiseman's Cove* and *Swashbuckler*, both of which were Book of the Year in the annual Children's Book Council of Australia awards. In 2001, *Touch Me* won the Victorian Premier's Prize for Young Adult Fiction.

James Moloney likes reading, eating, and the Brisbane Lions. He's fond of the New Zealand All Blacks too, but only when they lose to Australia at Rugby. James has never been chased by panthers but his kids made him take them to a theme park once and this book is his revenge.